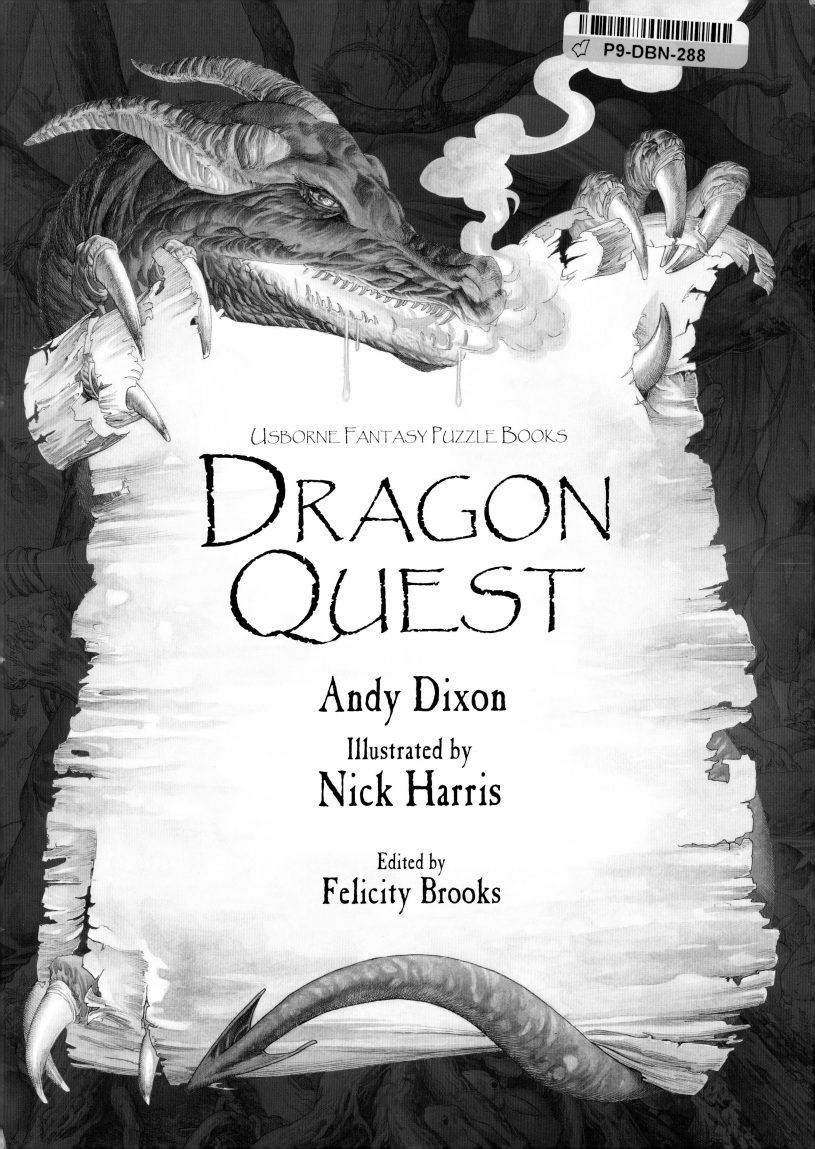

Usborne Fantasy Puzzle Books

Dragon Quest

Andy Dixon

Illustrated by
Nick Harris

Edited by
Felicity Brooks

Cover and additional design by
Amanda Gulliver and Stephanie Jones

Additional editing by Claire Masset

SHORTSVILLE NEEDS
YOU!

Citizens of Shortsville,

Once we were a happy, hairy people who had few problems and led easy lives. We joked and laughed. Our days were filled with joy. Then came the terrible day when a spell was cast over our village, an evil spell that made all our hair disappear! And we all know who was responsible for this callous crime. It was that spiteful, bald creature, Winston, the Wig-wearing Wizard. The time has come to put an end to his reign of terror. We must find and destroy the Well of Spells which is the source of his magic power. The journey will be long and dangerous and the well is guarded by a fearsome, fire-breathing dragon. So, citizens of Shortsville, I am looking for:

VOLUNTEERS TO GO ON THE DRAGON QUEST

If you think you are brave enough to face these challenges, then enter the Shortsville competitions and earn yourself a place on the quest.

Bag P. Dribbet

Mayor of Shortsville

Important information for all questers

Thank you for volunteering to go on the Dragon Quest, and welcome to the Land of Grandos. These are some things you need to know before you set off.

Your present location

You are in Shortsville, a village of little people in the Land of Grandos. The village is in the grip of a powerful spell cast by an evil wizard.

Your enemy

Your enemy is Winston, the Wig-wearing Wizard. He is a jealous and spiteful bald wizard who has recently cast a spell which made all of the villagers' hair fall out.

Your mission

The purpose of the quest is to find and destroy the Well of Spells which gives Winston all his magic power. The spell will be lifted as soon as the well is destroyed.

The Well of Spells

No one in Shortsville knows exactly where the Well of Spells is, but it is known to be guarded by a huge, fearsome dragon.

Your fellow questers

The three winners of the Shortsville competitions will go with you on the Dragon Quest. These competitions have been organized by Bag P. Dribbet, the Mayor of Shortsville. They are starting soon.

Time limit

Winter is approaching. The villagers need their hair to keep warm. Your mission must be accomplished as quickly as possible.

Your route

Your exact route is unknown, but you will set out from Shortsville and visit many other places in Grandos. The map below shows the whole of Grandos. Please study it carefully.

Octopus Ocean

Cadaver Castle

Sailor's Rest

Stinky Swamp

Trog Tower

Wingtip Rock

Misery Wood

Burning Rocks

Woodsman's Island

Shortsville

THE LAND OF GRANDOS

N
E
S

Old Mine

YOU ARE HERE

Temple of Fear

Tail End

Doomstones

The parchments

The quest will be difficult and dangerous, so you will need courage, cunning and the eyes of an eagle if you are to survive. In every place you visit you will see a piece of parchment similar to the one below. It contains vital information to get you safely through to the next stage of the quest.

Octopus Ocean

You have escaped from the ship into Octopus Ocean, where strange sea creatures lurk in every cavern and under every stone. Walking along the seabed is much too dangerous and slow, so you must find a faster and safer way to travel.

Someone has been here before you and left behind a small submarine. If you could make it work, it would be faster than walking, but the propeller is missing. Find the propeller and escape from the sea creatures.

Somewhere in the distance are 3 pipes which are sewer outlets from Cadaver Castle. Only one is safe to enter. The others are in use. Can you find some clues to show you which is the safe outlet?

Octopus Ocean has some of the largest and most valuable pearls in the world. Find 8 pearls. They may be useful later.

Most of the sea creatures are poisonous or too dangerous to catch. The crabs are safe to eat but they may give you a nasty nip. Find 6.

This tells you where you are.

These maps will help to remind you where each place is in Grandos. They come from an ancient book that belongs to the wise old man of Shortsville.

When it is time, read these pieces of information carefully. They contain some very important clues.

The pictures show people or things you have to find or avoid in each place you visit. Some will be very hard to spot, because you can only see a small part of them.

Some pictures show things you will need later in the quest or ways of getting to the next place.

At the bottom of the parchment are pictures of food or drink to look for. You can find something to eat in each place you visit.

The squares

At the bottom of each page are some more pictures in squares. The numbers tell you how many of that thing you can spot in the main scene. Finding these things will sharpen your skills and help you survive the quest.

11 seahorses

19 clownfish

Your enemy: Winston, the Wig-wearing Wizard

The red keys

Hidden in each of the first nine places you visit is one red key. You will need all nine later to help you defeat Winston, so don't forget to look for them.

The Shortsville competitions are about to begin. Turn the page to find out who will be going with you on the DRAGON QUEST...

Shortsville

The villagers of Shortsville are competing to find three people to go on the Dragon Quest. The judges are looking for people who are wise, brave and strong. The winners will go with you on your journey. Can you find them in the crowd?

Sprag wears glasses and a white shirt. He has a blue hat with spikes on it.

Dig always smiles. He wears a tiny red hat, a striped sweater and a shirt with a big white collar.

Pug wears an orange hat and a pink dress with yellow flowers. She hates ice cream.

To find your way, you'll need the book of maps. The wise old man of Shortsville is carrying it under his left arm. Can you find it?

There are all kinds of hidden dangers in Grandos, so you will need some weapons to protect yourselves. Can you find 4 swords, 2 axes and 2 shields?

You can't fight dragons on an empty stomach. You will need to take some food and drink. Find 7 bottles of yab's milk, 9 big bug burgers, and 9 tasty tarts.

10 snails

7 ice cream cones

9 buckets

22 judges

3 yabs

6 puppets

5 boxing gloves

Misery Wood

Your first stop is Misery Wood, a dark and dangerous place. There are six doors that lead out of the wood, but only one leads to safety. The other five will take you to Trog Tower from which there is no escape. Choose carefully or all is lost, and do not trust the rabbits.

The Trogs live in Trog Tower. They catch rabbits to put in their supper pot, but they prefer dwarves and humans. The Trogs are cowards. They always attack from behind, but if you shout "BOO!" at them, they'll run away. Find all 12 or they'll have you for supper.

The rabbits are mean and miserable creatures. They don't have any friends because they always tell lies. They know which door leads to safety, but when you ask them, they point the wrong way. Can you find all 34 rabbits and the safe door?

There is plenty of food in the woods, if you know what to look for. Find 9 apples, 10 wild mushrooms and fill your bottle from the stream.

9 birds

7 worms

5 moles

8

7 clubs   7 squirrels   16 flowers   5 owls   8 butterflies

9

Woodsman's Hut

You've escaped from Misery Wood and found your way to the woodsman's hut. The woodsman is very forgetful and his hut is so untidy that he can never find anything. Some weeks ago he lost something very important – the key to the clock that controls time.

This magical clock controls time in the woodsman's hut. When it stops, time stands still. To restore time, you must first find the clock and then the key to wind it.

 Key

Your next stop will be the Stinky Swamp. Many nasty creatures skulk in its murky depths. You need to find a boat and 2 oars to travel through the swamp.

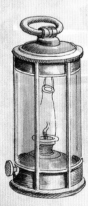

Night is falling fast. The swamp is the darkest place in Grandos. To light your way, you need to find a lantern and 7 candles.

There isn't much food here, but you are welcome to take 7 pieces of cheese. It's so smelly that even the mice won't touch it.

9 socks

9 ducks

6 hammers

6 saws

6 matchboxes

15 mice

6 pencils

7 paintbrushes

Stinky Swamp

Now you're in the middle of the swamp and the Frogmen are attacking your boat! You can't fight them off, so you need to distract them. Pug sees a huge model fly that has crashed in the water. If you can make it work, the Frogmen's frogs will chase it, as flies are the food they like best.

There are some parts missing from the engine in the fly's head. Find 3 batteries and 2 spark plugs to make it work.

The boat is filling up with water! Sprag pulled out the plug and threw it over the side by mistake. Can you find the plug before the boat sinks?

The frogmen keep their gold in the swamp. If you find 12 gold coins, you can hire a ship and its crew to take you to Cadaver Castle, the Wizard's home.

The only nice things in the Stinky Swamp are the purple cherries. Some grow as big as basketballs. There are 8 cherries to find.

6 tadpoles

8 herons

8 otters

9 grubs 9 piranhas 5 skulls 9 snakes 10 terrapins

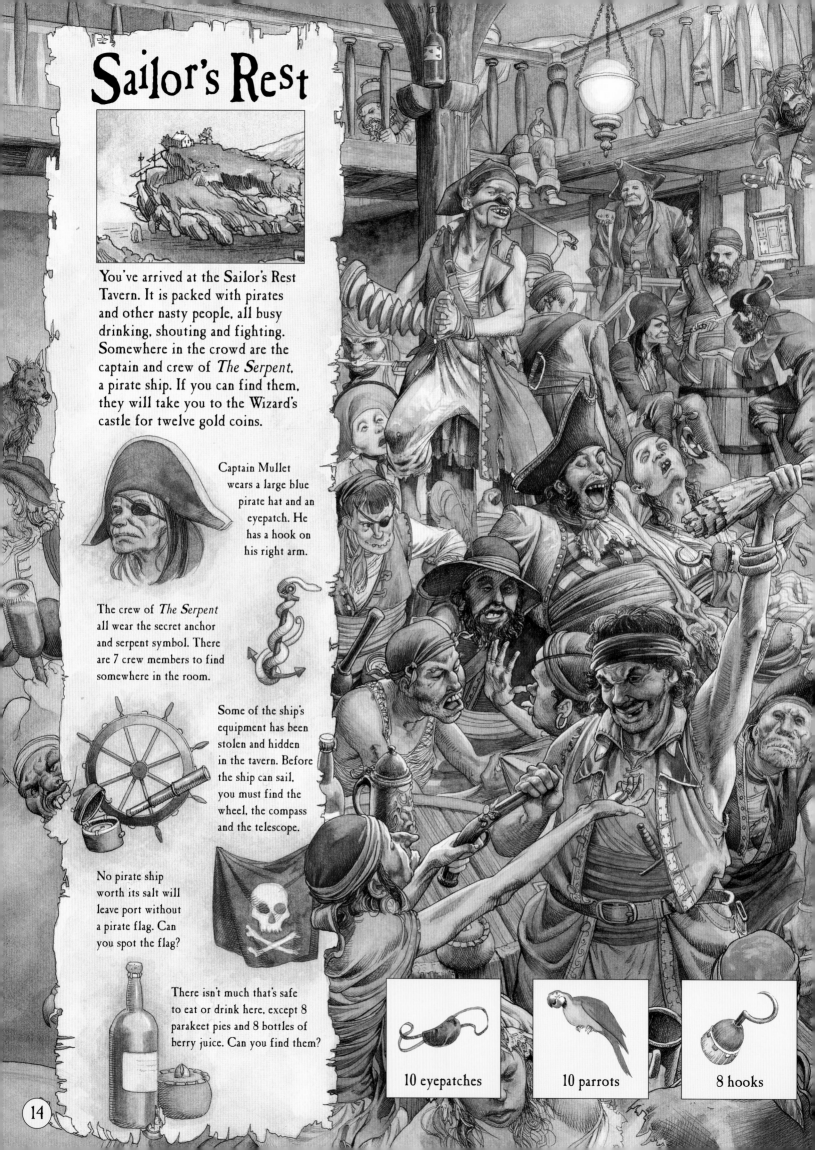

Sailor's Rest

You've arrived at the Sailor's Rest Tavern. It is packed with pirates and other nasty people, all busy drinking, shouting and fighting. Somewhere in the crowd are the captain and crew of *The Serpent*, a pirate ship. If you can find them, they will take you to the Wizard's castle for twelve gold coins.

Captain Mullet wears a large blue pirate hat and an eyepatch. He has a hook on his right arm.

The crew of *The Serpent* all wear the secret anchor and serpent symbol. There are 7 crew members to find somewhere in the room.

Some of the ship's equipment has been stolen and hidden in the tavern. Before the ship can sail, you must find the wheel, the compass and the telescope.

No pirate ship worth its salt will leave port without a pirate flag. Can you spot the flag?

There isn't much that's safe to eat or drink here, except 8 parakeet pies and 8 bottles of berry juice. Can you find them?

10 eyepatches

10 parrots

8 hooks

14

5 wooden legs

6 watches

9 cutlasses

5 treasure maps

23 playing cards

The Serpent

The evil Captain Mullet has locked you in the hold of the ship. He must be working for the Wizard! There is some old diving equipment in the hold. If you put it on, you can sink *The Serpent* and escape when the captain and his crew abandon ship.

There are 4 diving helmets, 4 oxygen tanks, and 4 pairs of heavy divers' boots to find somewhere in the hold of the ship. The boots will stop you from floating up to the surface of the sea when you escape into the ocean.

When it's time to sink *The Serpent*, you'll need to pull out the ship's large plug. Can you see where it is?

There are some very dangerous creatures at the bottom of the ocean. You should take some harpoon guns for protection. There are 4 to find.

Before you put on the diving suits and pull the plug, you'll need something to eat. See if you can find 12 bananas and 12 crackers.

6 anchors

10 pigs

5 lobster pots

10 cannon balls

11 chickens

7 fishing reels

7 barrels

Octopus Ocean

You've escaped from the ship into Octopus Ocean, where strange sea creatures lurk in every cavern and under every stone. Walking along the seabed is much too dangerous and slow, so you must find a faster and safer way to travel.

Someone has been here before you and left a small submarine behind. If you could make it work, it would be faster than walking, but the propeller is missing. Find the propeller and escape from the sea creatures.

Somewhere in the distance are 3 pipes which are sewer outlets from Cadaver Castle. Only one is safe to enter. The others are in use. Can you find some clues to show you which is the safe outlet?

Octopus Ocean has some of the largest and most valuable pearls in the world. Find 8 pearls. They may be useful later.

Most of the sea creatures are poisonous or too dangerous to catch. The crabs are safe to eat, but they may give you a nasty nip. Find 6.

8 octopuses

19 clownfish

6 eels

12 sea urchins   8 sharks   11 seahorses   10 starfish   5 giant clams

Smelly Sewers

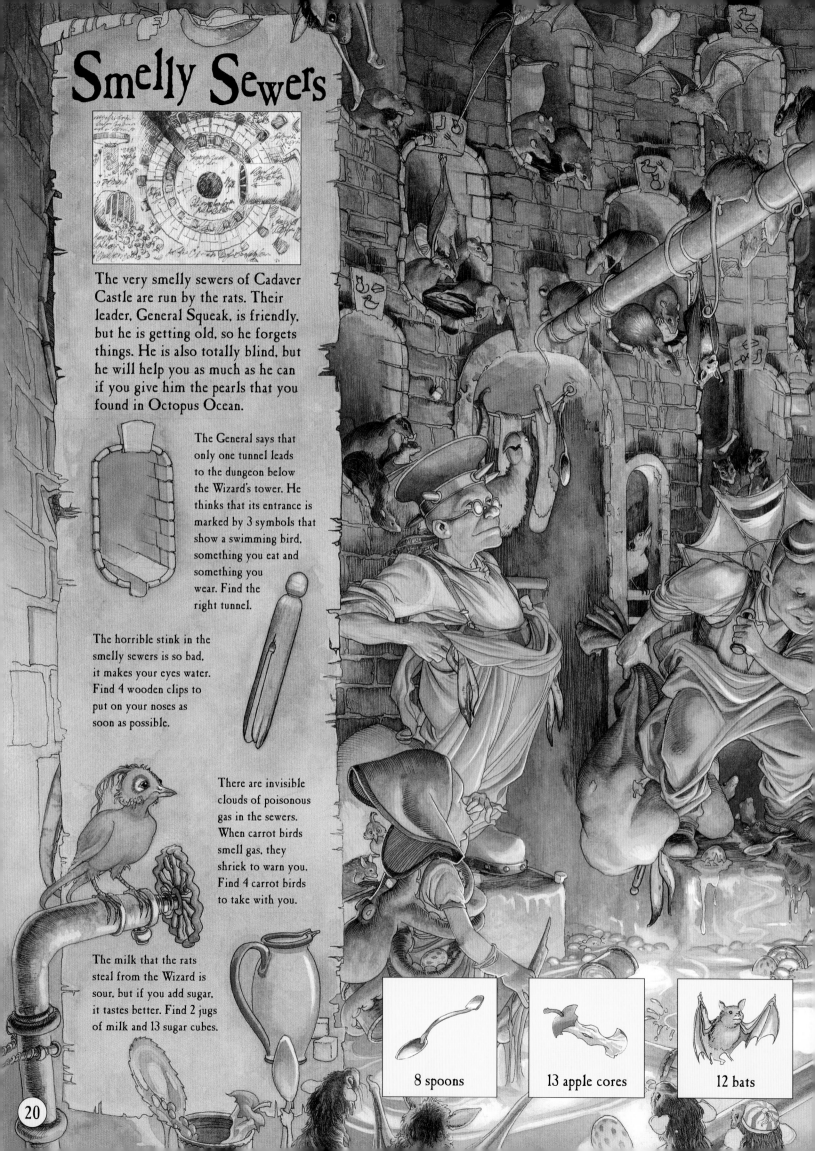

The very smelly sewers of Cadaver Castle are run by the rats. Their leader, General Squeak, is friendly, but he is getting old, so he forgets things. He is also totally blind, but he will help you as much as he can if you give him the pearls that you found in Octopus Ocean.

The General says that only one tunnel leads to the dungeon below the Wizard's tower. He thinks that its entrance is marked by 3 symbols that show a swimming bird, something you eat and something you wear. Find the right tunnel.

The horrible stink in the smelly sewers is so bad, it makes your eyes water. Find 4 wooden clips to put on your noses as soon as possible.

There are invisible clouds of poisonous gas in the sewers. When carrot birds smell gas, they shriek to warn you. Find 4 carrot birds to take with you.

The milk that the rats steal from the Wizard is sour, but if you add sugar, it tastes better. Find 2 jugs of milk and 13 sugar cubes.

8 spoons

13 apple cores

12 bats

11 bones

15 teabags

15 rotten eggs

11 tin cans

19 banana skins

Giant's Kitchen

You've escaped from the smelly sewers into a kitchen, where a giant grabs hold of Pug. He says that he and his wife are exhausted. They've been slaving away all day for the Wizard, who has been ringing for food from his tower. Now they are too tired to make their own supper, but the giant is hungry. He won't let go of Pug unless you make him a hot meal.

The giant wants a mushroom omelette. All the ingredients are somewhere in the kitchen. Find some butter, a bottle of yab's milk, 6 eggs and 9 mushrooms.

The next place you visit will be the Spellroom in the tower. The Wizard has many large and nasty cats. Take some cans of cat food and a can opener to keep them happy. There are 8 cans to find.

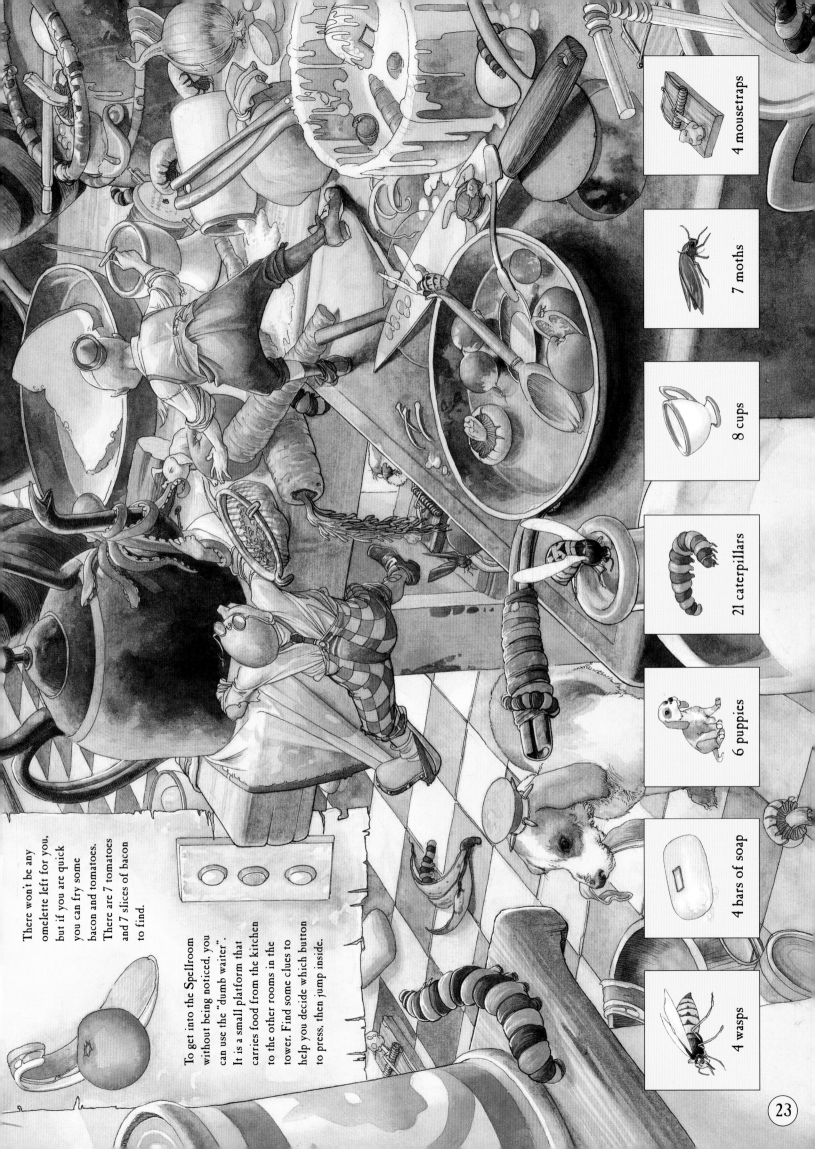

There won't be any omelette left for you, but if you are quick you can fry some bacon and tomatoes. There are 7 tomatoes and 7 slices of bacon to find.

To get into the Spellroom without being noticed, you can use the "dumb waiter". It is a small platform that carries food from the kitchen to the other rooms in the tower. Find some clues to help you decide which button to press, then jump inside.

4 mousetraps

7 moths

8 cups

21 caterpillars

6 puppies

4 bars of soap

4 wasps

The Spellroom

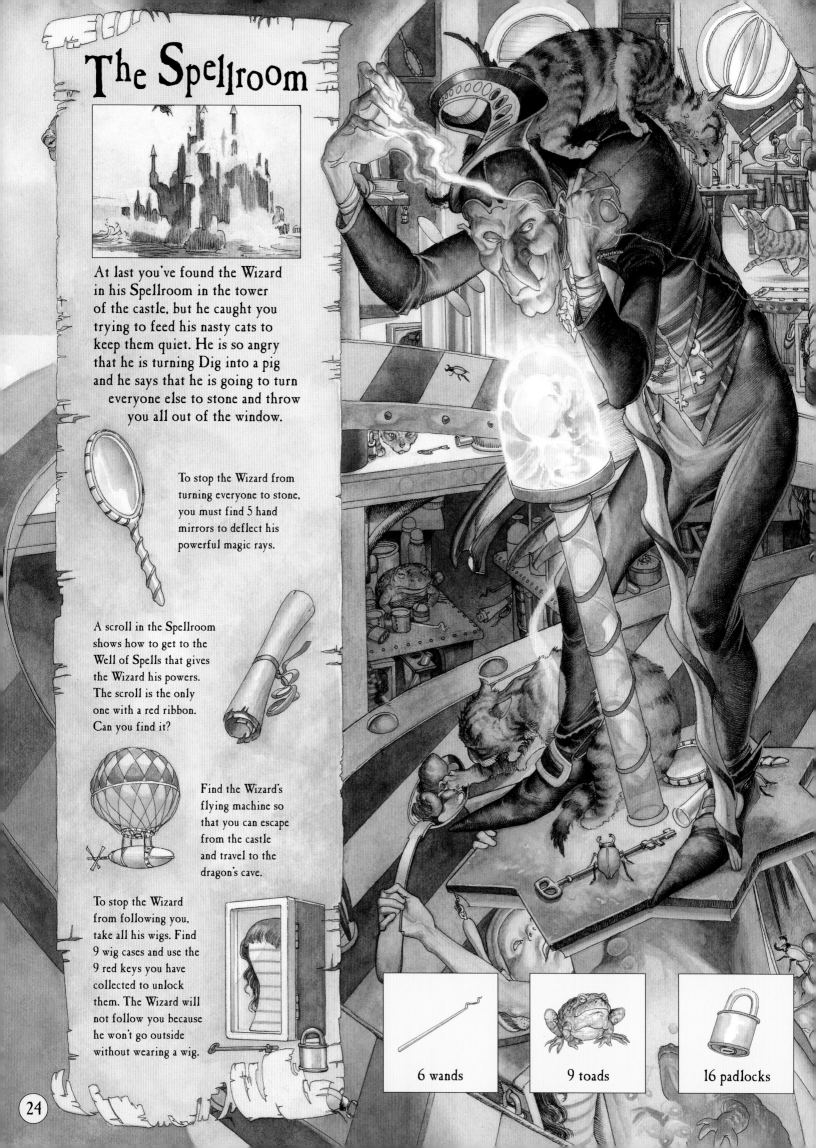

At last you've found the Wizard in his Spellroom in the tower of the castle, but he caught you trying to feed his nasty cats to keep them quiet. He is so angry that he is turning Dig into a pig and he says that he is going to turn everyone else to stone and throw you all out of the window.

To stop the Wizard from turning everyone to stone, you must find 5 hand mirrors to deflect his powerful magic rays.

A scroll in the Spellroom shows how to get to the Well of Spells that gives the Wizard his powers. The scroll is the only one with a red ribbon. Can you find it?

Find the Wizard's flying machine so that you can escape from the castle and travel to the dragon's cave.

To stop the Wizard from following you, take all his wigs. Find 9 wig cases and use the 9 red keys you have collected to unlock them. The Wizard will not follow you because he won't go outside without wearing a wig.

6 wands

9 toads

16 padlocks

18 beetles   6 brushes   10 cats   7 hourglasses

Dragon's Cave

You've finally reached the dragon's cave, deep inside an old gold mine. Winston discovered it years ago while digging for gold. He found that if he kept drinking the water from the Well of Spells it turned him into a great wizard. Now's your chance to defeat the huge dragon, destroy the well and then make your escape.

Your swords are useless against the dragon's scaly skin. Find the pump handle and the hose to pump water from the well into the dragon's mouth. If you put out his fire he won't be able to fight, and will run away.

The railway track leads back to the entrance of the mine which is near Shortsville. The wagon is powered by a small motor. Find 6 lamps and pour the fuel from them into the motor to get it working so that you can escape.

Find 7 sticks of dynamite and the detonator to blow up the cave. When you have done this, the well will be destroyed, the spell will be lifted, everyone's hair will grow again and Dig will return to normal.

7 pickaxes

12 fossils

16 lizards

6 buckets 4 lances 5 helmets 5 shovels

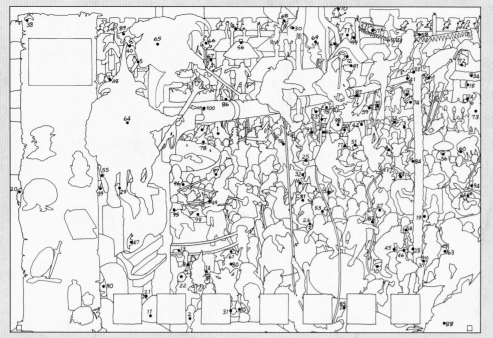

Shortsville 6-7

Sprag 1

Dig 2

Pug 3

Book of maps 4

Swords 5 6 7 8

Axes 9 10

Shields 11 12

Bottles of yab's milk 13 14 15
16 17 18 19

Big bug burgers 20 21 22
23 24 25 26 27 28

Tasty tarts 29 30 31 32 33
34 35 36 37

Snails 38 39 40 41 42 43
44 45 46 47

Ice cream cones 48 49 50
51 52 53 54

Buckets 55 56 57 58 59 60
61 62 63

Judges 64 65 66 67 68 69
70 71 72 73 74 75 76 77
78 79 80 81 82 83 84 85

Yabs 86 87 88

Puppets 89 90 91 92 93 94

Boxing gloves 95 96 97
98 99

Red key 100

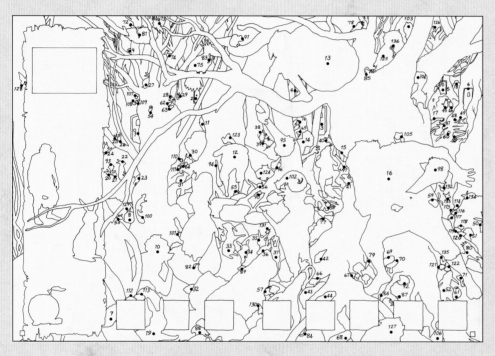

Misery Wood 8-9

Doors 1 2 3 4 5 6

Trogs 7 8 9 10 11 12 13 14
15 16 17 18

Rabbits 19 20 21 22 23 24
25 26 27 28 29 30 31 32
33 34 35 36 37 38 39 40
41 42 43 44 45 46 47 48
49 50 51 52

Apples 53 54 55 56 57 58
59 60 61

Mushrooms 62 63 64 65 66
67 68 69 70 71

Birds 72 73 74 75 76 77 78
79 80

Worms 81 82 83 84 85
86 87

Moles 88 89 90 91 92

Clubs 93 94 95 96 97
98 99

Squirrels 100 101 102 103
104 105 106

Flowers 107 108 109 110
111 112 113 114 115 116 117
118 119 120 121 122

Owls 123 124 125 126 127

Butterflies 128 129 130 131
132 133 134 135

Red key 136

The door that leads
to safety is door 5

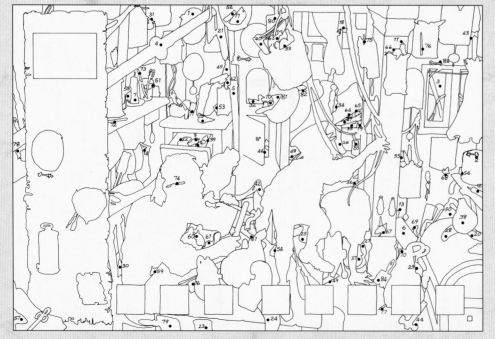

Woodsman's Hut 10-11

Clock 1

Magic key 2

Boat 3

Oars 4 5

Lantern 6

Candles 7 8 9 10 11 12 13

Cheeses 14 15 16 17 18
19 20

Socks 21 22 23 24 25 26
27 28 29

Ducks 30 31 32 33 34 35
36 37 38

Hammers 39 40 41 42
43 44

Saws 45 46 47 48 49 50

Matchboxes 51 52 53 54
55 56

Mice 57 58 59 60 61 62 63
64 65 66 67 68 69 70 71

Pencils 72 73 74 75 76 77

Paintbrushes 78 79 80 81
82 83 84

Red key 85

Stinky Swamp 12–13

Batteries 1 2 3

Spark plugs 4 5

Plug 6

Gold coins 7 8 9 10 11 12
13 14 15 16 17 18

Cherries 19 20 21 22 23
24 25 26

Tadpoles 27 28 29 30
31 32

Herons 33 34 35 36 37 38
39 40

Otters 41 42 43 44 45 46
47 48

Grubs 49 50 51 52 53 54
55 56 57

Piranhas 58 59 60 61 62
63 64 65 66

Skulls 67 68 69 70 71

Snakes 73 74 75 76 77 78
79 80 81

Terrapins 82 83 84 85 86
87 88 89 90 91

Red key 92

Sailor's Rest 14–15

Captain Mullet 1

Anchor and serpent
symbols 2 3 4 5 6 7 8

Wheel 9

Compass 10

Telescope 11

Flag 12

Parakeet pies 13 14 15 16
17 18 19 20

Berry juice 21 22 23 24 25
26 27 28

Eyepatches 29 30 31 32
33 34 35 36 37 38

Parrots 39 40 41 42 43 44
45 46 47 48

Hooks 49 50 51 52 53 54
55 56

Wooden legs 57 58 59
60 61

Watches 62 63 64 65
66 67

Cutlasses 68 69 70 71 72
73 74 75 76

Treasure maps 77 78 79
80 81

Playing cards 82 83 84 85
86 87 88 89 90 91 92
93 94 95 96 97 98 99
100 101 102 103 104

Red key 105

The Serpent 16–17

Helmets 1 2 3 4

Oxygen tanks 5 6 7 8

Boots 9 10 11 12 13 14
15 16

Plug 17

Harpoons 18 19
20 21

Bananas 22 23 24 25
26 27 28 29 30 31
32 33

Crackers 34 35 36 37
38 39 40 41 42 43
44 45

Anchors 46 47 48 49
50 51

Pigs 52 53 54 55 56
57 58 59 60 61

Lobster pots 62 63 64
65 66

Cannon balls 67 68
69 70 71 72 73 74
75 76

Chickens 77 78 79
80 81 82 83 84 85
86 87

Fishing reels 88 89 90
91 92 93 94

Barrels 95 96 97 98
99 100 101

Red key 102

Octopus Ocean 18–19

Submarine 1

Propeller 2

Sewer pipe clues 3 4

Correct pipe 5

Pearls 6 7 8 9 10 11 12 13

Crabs 14 15 16 17 18 19

Octopuses 20 21 22 23 24
 25 26 27

Clownfish 28 29 30 31 32
 33 34 35 36 37 38 39 40
 41 42 43 44 45 46

Eels 47 48 49 50 51 52

Sea urchins 53 54 55 56 57
 58 59 60 61 62 63 64

Sharks 65 66 67 68 69 70
 71 72

Seahorses 73 74 75 76 77
 78 79 80 81 82 83

Starfish 84 85 86 87 88 89
 90 91 92 93

Giant clams 94 95 96 97 98

Red key 99

Smelly Sewers 20–21

Correct tunnel 1

Wooden clips 2 3 4 5

Carrot birds 6 7 8 9

Jugs of milk 10 11

Sugar cubes 12 13 14 15 16
 17 18 19 20 21 22 23 24

Spoons 25 26 27 28 29 30
 31 32

Apple cores 33 34 35 36 37
 38 39 40 41 42 43 44 45

Bats 46 47 48 49 50 51 52
 53 54 55 56 57

Bones 58 59 60 61 62 63
 64 65 66 67 68

Teabags 69 70 71 72 73
 74 75 76 77 78 79 80 81
 82 83

Rotten eggs 84 85 86 87 88
 89 90 91 92 93 94 95 96
 97 98

Tin cans 99 100 101 102
 103 104 105 106 107
 108 109

Banana skins 110 111 112 113
 114 115 116 117 118 119
 120 121 122 123 124 125
 126 127 128

Red key 129

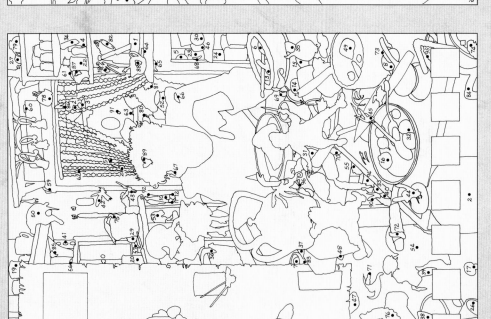

Giant's Kitchen 22–23

Butter 1

Bottle of yab's milk 2

Eggs 3 4 5 6 7 8

Mushrooms 9 10 11 12 13 14
 15 16 17

Can opener 18

Cans of cat food 19 20 21
 22 23 24 25 26

Tomatoes 27 28 29 30 31
 32 33

Slices of bacon 34 35 36 37
 38 39 40

Correct button 41 (It's dirty
because giant presses it to
send food up to tower, and
middle bell that wizard rings
has no cobwebs on it.)

Wasps 42 43 44 45

Soap 46 47 48 49

Puppies 50 51 52 53 54 55

Caterpillars 56 57 58 59 60
 61 62 63 64 65 66 67 68
 69 70 71 72 73 74 75 76

Cups 77 78 79 80 81 82
 83 84

Moths 85 86 87 88 89
 90 91

Mousetraps 92 93 94 95

Red key 96

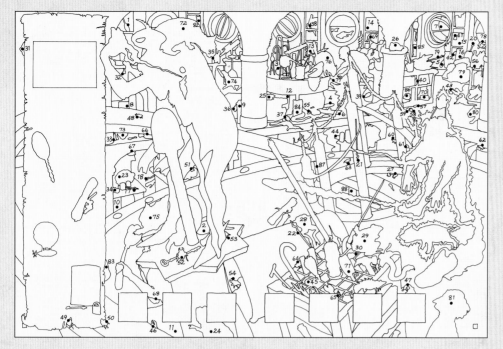

The Spellroom 24-25

Mirrors 1 2 3 4 5

Scroll with red ribbon 6

Flying machine 7

Wig cases 8 9 10 11 12 13
   14 15 16

Wands 17 18 19 20 21 22

Toads 23 24 25 26 27 28
   29 30 31

Padlocks 32 33 34 35 36
   37 38 39 40 41 42 43
   44 45 46 47

Beetles 48 49 50 51 52 53
   54 55 56 57 58 59 60
   61 62 63 64 65

Brushes 66 67 68 69
   70 71

Cats 72 73 74 75 76 77
   78 79 80 81

Hourglasses 82 83 84 85
   86 87 88

Dragon's Cave 26-27

Pump handle 1

Hose 2

Lamps 3 4 5 6 7 8

Detonator 9

Sticks of dynamite 10 11 12
   13 14 15 16

Pickaxes 17 18 19 20 21
   22 23

Fossils 24 25 26 27 28 29
   30 31 32 33 34 35

Lizards 36 37 38 39 40 41
   42 43 44 45 46 47 48
   49 50 51

Buckets 52 53 54 55
   56 57

Lances 58 59 60 61

Shovels 62 63 64 65 66

Helmets 67 68 69 70 71

Extra puzzles

1. GRANDOS is an anagram – if you rearrange the
letters it makes another word. What is it?

2. The Land of Grandos, shown on the map on page 4,
is the shape of one of the creatures in this book.
Can you see which one?

(Answers are upside down at the bottom of this page.)

Can you find?

~ a bird's nest and a ginger cat in Shortsville?

~ a parachuting mole in Misery Wood?

~ a small photograph in the Woodsman's Hut?

~ a waterskiing terrapin in the Stinky Swamp?

~ an eyeball in the Sailor's Rest?

~ three mice in a lifeboat in *The Serpent*?

~ a clownfish with a hat and a parrot with
a snorkel in Octopus Ocean?

~ two rats with hats in the Stinky Sewers?

~ a sleeping bat in the Giant's Kitchen?

~ two snakes and two fish in the Spellroom?

~ a sunbathing lizard in the Dragon's Cave?

Goodbye!